For E: ad astra, my darling girl!
—A.H.

For Kirsty,
without whom I'd never have
reached for the stars
—G.E.O.

Girls Belong in Space
Text copyright © 2025 by Ashlee Hashman
Illustrations copyright © 2025 by Gillian Eilidh O'Mara
All rights reserved. Manufactured in Capriate San Gervasio, Italy.
No part of this book may be used or reproduced in any manner whatsoever
without written permission except in the case of brief quotations
embodied in critical articles and reviews. For information address
HarperCollins Children's Books, a division of HarperCollins Publishers,
195 Broadway, New York, NY 10007.
www.harpercollinschildrens.com

Library of Congress Control Number: 2024944527
ISBN 978-0-06-324784-0

The artist used a mixture of ink, paint, digital art, and stardust
to create the illustrations for this book.
Typography by Honee Jang
24 25 26 27 28 RTLO 10 9 8 7 6 5 4 3 2 1
First Edition

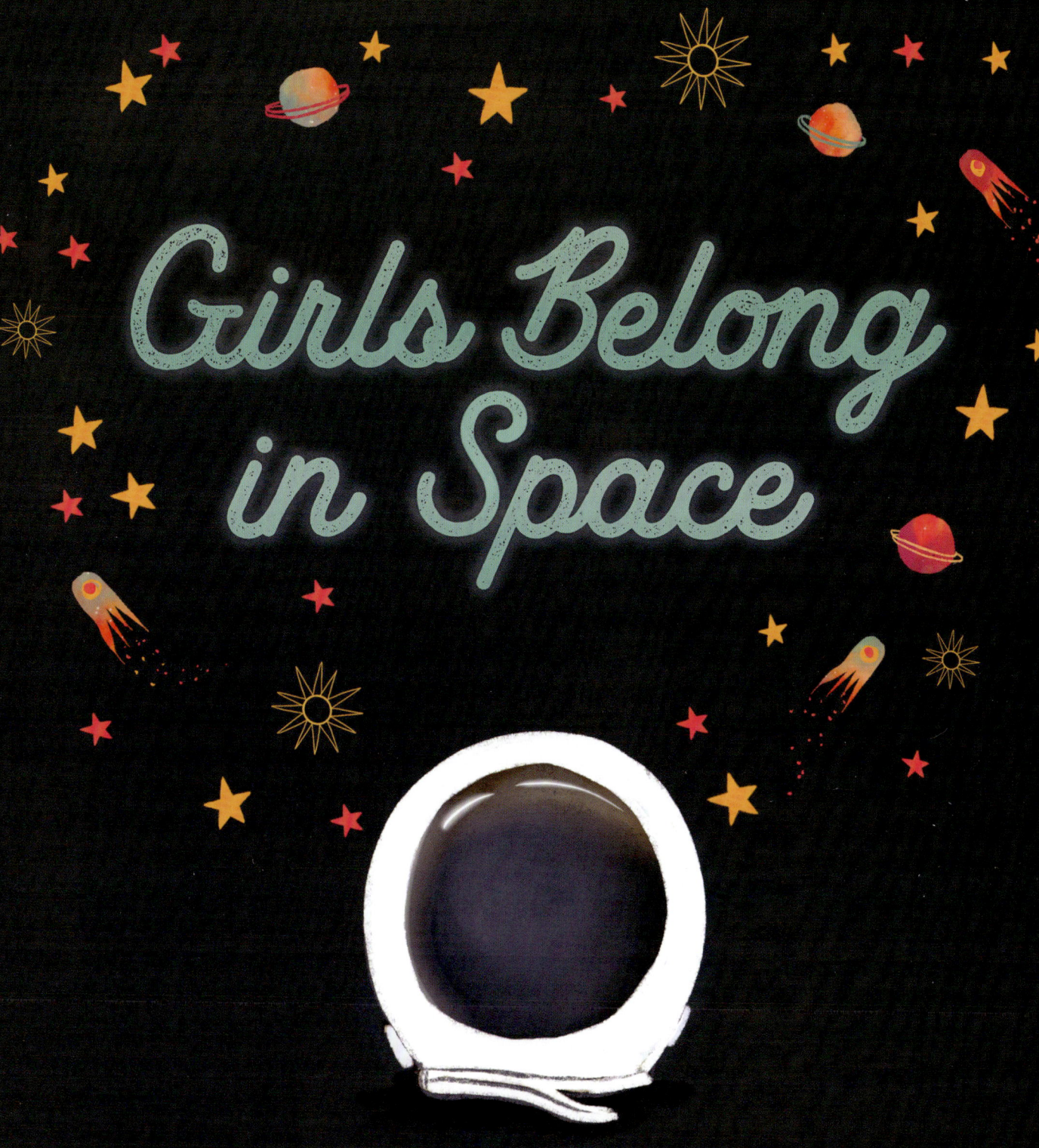

Girls Belong in Space

written by
Ashlee Hashman

illustrated by
Gillian Eilidh O'Mara

HARPER
An Imprint of HarperCollinsPublishers

Planets have orbits.
Each star has a place.
But where do girls fit
in infinite space?

They count and they calculate
faster than light,

which is why girls belong
where the stars glow at night.

They run and they lift to get strong and fit,

Judith Resnik

which is why girls belong
in a shuttle's cockpit.

In science and physics,
their grades are outstanding,

Christina Hammock Koch

which is why girls belong at a major moon landing.

which is why girls belong
in gleaming space suits.

Incredible pilots,
they zoom, soar, and veer,
which is why girls belong
on the final frontier.

Eileen Collins

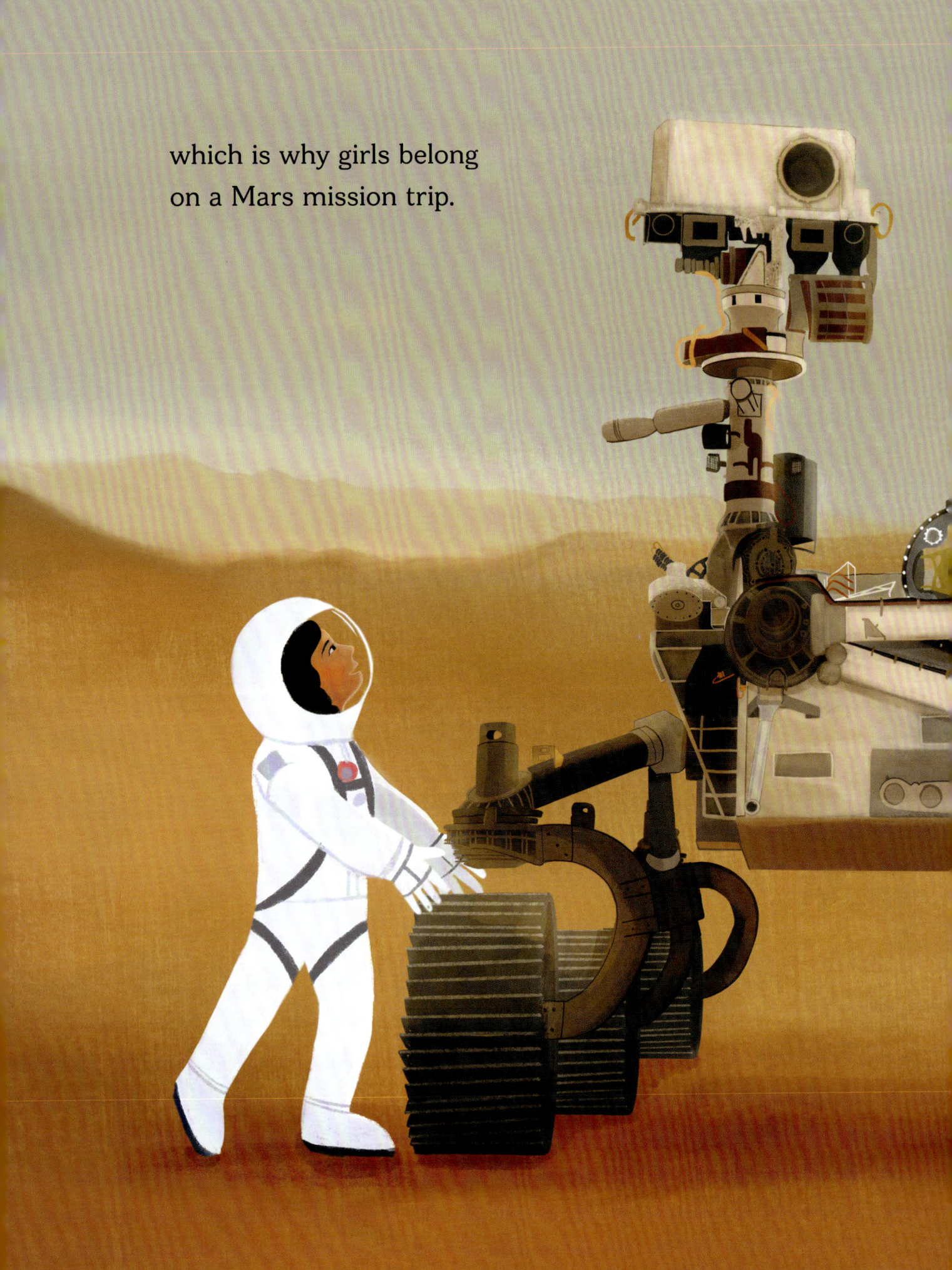

which is why girls belong on a Mars mission trip.

They've dreamed all their lives
of zero-g dances,
which is why girls belong
in the sky, taking chances.

Sally Ride

Girls rise to the challenge, stare fear in the face . . .

. . . which is why girls are perfect
for shining in space.

Did you know?

By the time you have read this book from start to finish (about five minutes):

- Earth will have traveled about 5,550 miles in its orbit around the sun
- nearly one million stars will be born
- Neptune may experience a "rainstorm" with giant diamonds instead of rain
- three hundred tons of gases and particles will erupt from volcanoes on Jupiter's moon Io
- more than six hundred baby girls will be born, some of them future astronauts!

If you are curious about space, you are in the company of the most brilliant minds in history! The moment I became interested in space travel was during a third-grade field trip to the local science center. We were assigned special roles to complete a "real" lunar landing. I'll never forget the feeling of piloting that pretend shuttle to get our team safely to the moon! I felt so incredibly big and so impossibly small at the same time. In that moment, I fell in love with space and wanted to know more about the women who explored it.

This book is meant to honor the brave women who have made space exploration possible. Before they were cosmic adventurers, though, they were curious kids . . . like YOU! So go forth and explore!

—Ashlee Hashman

Women in Space

Katherine Johnson was a brilliant African American mathematician whose quick calculations helped NASA put the nation's first astronauts into orbit.

Dr. Judith Resnik was the first Jewish American astronaut. She went through rigorous training to take part in the *Discovery* and *Challenger* flights. Her contributions to the fields of electrical engineering and biomedical research were vital to the orbiter missions.

Christina Hammock Koch is an American astronaut who holds the record for longest single spaceflight by a woman (328 days). She has taken part in six spacewalks, including the first all-female spacewalk, and is set to be the first woman to orbit the moon during the Artemis missions.

Dr. Ellen Ochoa became the first Latine woman to go into space aboard the shuttle *Discovery*. She has been in space a total of four times and moved on to become the eleventh director of Johnson Space Center.

Native New Yorker **Colonel Eileen Collins**'s journey into space began when a new class of astronauts (including women!) visited her air force base. When speaking of her achievements as the first female shuttle pilot and commander of the *Columbia* STS-93 mission, Collins said, "The young people are going to be the ones to take us on to more exciting adventures."

Dr. Sally Ride was an astronaut and physicist who became the first American woman in space. She worked the robotic arm on the STS-7 space shuttle mission and helped put satellites into orbit. After leaving NASA, Sally devoted her life to helping girls pursue their interests in science and math.

During the 2020 *Perseverance* mission, a team of exceptional women guided the rover to Mars. The team included:

Heather Ann Bottom
(systems engineer)

Vandana "Vandi" Verma
(senior engineer and rover driver)

Michelle Tomey Colizzi
(aeroshell vehicle lead)

Diana Trujillo
(technical group supervisor for sequence planning and execution and tactical mission lead)

Kathryn Stack Morgan
(deputy project scientist)

Swati Mohan
(lead guidance, navigation, and controls engineer)

Moogega Cooper
(planetary protection lead)

Further Readings

Becker, Helaine. *Counting on Katherine: How Katherine Johnson Saved Apollo 13*. New York: Henry Holt and Co, 2018.

Klepeis, Alicia. *Gutsy Girls Go For Science: Astronauts*. Norwich, VT: Nomad Press, 2019.

NASA. "Women at NASA." www.nasa.gov/women-at-nasa.

———. "NASA Lewis Welcomed Judy Resnik, One of First Female Astronauts." www.nasa.gov/history/nasa-lewis-welcomed-judy-resnik-one-of-first-female-astronauts.

National Women's Hall of Fame. "Eileen Collins." www.womenofthehall.org/inductee/eileen-collins.

Rappaport, Doreen. *Ellen Takes Flight: The Life of Astronaut Ellen Ochoa*. New York: Little, Brown Books for Young Readers, 2023.

Sanchez Vegara, Maria Isabel. *Sally Ride*. London: Frances Lincoln Children's Books, 2024.